Rugrats in Paris THE MOVIE

Tommy's Bestest Adventure

Adapted by Becky Gold
Based on the Script by
David N. Weiss & J. David Stem
and Jill Gorey & Barbara Herndon
and Kate Boutilier

Illustrated by Studio Orlando

Simon Spotlight/Nickelodeon

New York   London   Toronto   Sydney   Singapore

Based on the TV series *Rugrats*® created by Arlene Klasky, Gabor Csupo, and
Paul Germain as seen on Nickelodeon®

SIMON SPOTLIGHT
An imprint of Simon & Schuster Children's Publishing Division
1230 Avenue of the Americas
New York, New York 10020

Manufactured in the United States of America

First Edition

2 4 6 8 10 9 7 5 3 1

ISBN 0-689-83426-8

Hi, I'm Tommy. Guess where I gots to go? On the bestest adventure to the bestest place in the whole world—Reptarland!

Reptarland is in Parrots, France. That's very far away. We had to take a plane to get there!

But first we had to get our past-poor pictures taken. Angelica said hers was the prettiest.

Then we went up in the plane. I liked helpin' fly it, 'cept when the plane got the hiccups.

Phil and Lil went lookin' for stuff. And Angelica tried talkin' francy to a stewer-desk ('cause people in France speak francy).

At last we gots to Parrots!

We stayed in a hotel in Reptarland that had alligators. Chuckie didn't want to ride 'em, but I told him they don't bite.

The beds were nice and bouncy too. And there was a potty that squirted back!

A mean lady named Coco told my daddy to fix Reptar. We sawed Reptar's head in her office. We just had to find the rest of him!

Coco got really mad when she sawed us. "Do something!" she told her helper Jean-Claude. She didn't like us at all. But Angelica liked her a lot.

Then Coco's other helper, a nice lady named Kira, took us to the Princess Parade. See, Reptarland gots a princess. The princess helps everybodies not to be afraid of Reptar.

The minute Chuckie saw the princess, he knowed he wanted her to be his mommy. She was better than all his daddy's poopy dates—'specially Coco.

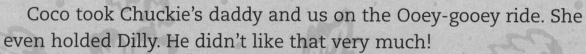

Coco took Chuckie's daddy and us on the Ooey-gooey ride. She even holded Dilly. He didn't like that very much!

Kira's little girl, Kimi, came too. She helped us find the princess's castle in the bowlcano! Kimi knowed the park like the back of her ham.

But at the bowlcano, some big, angry men chased us. When we came to the castle, Chuckie was too a-scared to knock on the door. So he didn't get to meet the princess, till . . .

the Princess Speck-dacular! We was so egg-sited, till we found out the princess was really that meanie Coco! She tooked Chuckie's Wawa bear.

But Chuckie's daddy fell under her smell. "Chuckie and I are in love with Coco!" he said. He was gonna marry Coco!

Chuckie was gonna get a mommy, all right . . . but not the kinda mommy he wanted. I never seed him so sad afore.

Coco didn't want us at the wedding. She made Jean-Claude take us to a cold, yucky place. Then Angelica told us that she helped that mean lady marry Chuckie's daddy!

"We gots to stop her!" Chuckie shouted.

Reptar to the rescue! At first we didn't know how to make him go.

When we finally did, Reptar had to fight off Robosnail. When all the fightin' was over, we had to find the place where Chuckie's daddy was gettin' married.

Just in time we made it to the church and saved Chuckie's daddy from Coco!

And guess what happened? Everything worked out okeydokey 'cause . . .

Chuckie's daddy married Kira! Chuckie gots a great mommy and sister. And I gots a brand-new friend!